This book belongs to

_____

The Steadfast Tin Soldier

BY

Hans Christian Andersen

Retold by Samantha Easton

ILLUSTRATED BY

Michael Montgomery

ARIEL BOOKS

ANDREWS AND McMEEL
KANSAS CITY

Library of Congress Cataloging-in-Publication Data

Easton, Samantha.
    The steadfast tin soldier / Hans Christian Andersen ; retold by
Samantha Easton ; illustrated by Michael Montgomery.
        p.   cm.
    Summary: The perilous adventure of a toy soldier who loves a paper
dancing girl culminates in tragedy for both of them.
    ISBN 0-8362-4929-1 : $6.95
    [1. Fairy tales. 2. Toys—Fiction.] I. Montgomery, Michael,
1952–   ill. II. Andersen, H. C. (Hans Christian), 1805–1875.
Standhaftige tinsoldat. III. Title.
PZ8.E135St   1991
[E]—dc20   91–10990
                                                         CIP
                                                          AC

Design: Susan Hood and Mike Hortens
Art Direction: Armand Eisen, Mike Hortens, and Julie Phillips
Art Production: Lynn Wine
Production: Julie Miller and Lisa Shadid

The Steadfast
Tin Soldier

*O*nce upon a time there were twenty-five
toy tin soldiers. They were brothers, for they
had all been made from the same tin spoon.
They wore fine red and blue uniforms and
carried little guns, and they all lived together
in a carved wooden box.

The first words they ever heard came
from a little boy as he lifted the lid off their
wooden box. "Oh look!" the boy cried. "Tin
soldiers!"

7

It was the boy's birthday and he
had been given the tin soldiers as
a present. Clapping his hands
with delight, the boy set the tin
soldiers on the table. They
were all exactly alike except for
one who had but one leg. He had been made
last and there had not been enough tin left
to finish him properly.

Besides the soldiers, the table was covered
with all sorts of wonderful toys. The prettiest
was a paper castle.

This castle was so beautifully made that through its windows could be seen little rooms complete with tiny paper furniture and tapestries. In front of the castle little paper trees stood around a small mirror that was meant to be a lake. And on the mirror lake swam tiny wax swans. All this was very lovely, but the loveliest part of the castle was a tiny dancer who stood in the castle door.

The dancer, too, was made of paper. She wore a dress of white tulle. A little blue ribbon was wrapped like a shawl around her shoulders. This ribbon was held in place with a silver sequin the same size as her face.

The little dancer's arms gracefully stretched out in front of her, and one of her legs was raised so high behind her that the little tin soldier could not see it.

"She must have only one leg, just as I do!" he thought. "How pretty she is! She would make me the perfect wife!" Then he thought sadly, "But she is far too grand for me. She lives in a fine castle, while I live in a wooden box that I share with my brothers. Still, I must try to get to know her!"

So the little tin soldier stretched out on the table behind a snuffbox. From there he could watch the little dancer.

When evening came, the little boy put all the other tin soldiers back in their wooden box. Then the people of the house turned out the lights and went to bed.

When the people were asleep, the toys came to life and began to amuse themselves. They visited with each other and danced and played all sorts of games. The dolls waltzed. The teddy bears played leapfrog. The colored pencils chased each other over the drawing pad. And the cuckoo in the clock sang a lively song.

The tin soldiers rattled the lid of their box for they wished to get out and join the fun. Only the tin soldier and the little dancer stayed still. She stood on tiptoe in the castle door and held one leg stretched out behind her as steadily as the tin soldier stood on his one leg. The little tin soldier stared at the little dancer and she stared back, but neither of them spoke.

At the stroke of midnight, the lid of the snuffbox sprang open, and out popped a little red goblin.

"Tin soldier," growled the goblin. "You will please remember to keep your eyes to yourself!"

But the tin soldier pretended not to hear. Then the goblin said in a nasty voice, "Very well. I'll take care of you tomorrow!" With that he disappeared into the snuffbox.

Early the next morning, the little boy came running into the room with his brother. They picked up the little tin soldier and set him on the windowsill. Now, I don't know whether it was the red goblin's doing or not, but just then a strong gust of wind blew the little tin soldier off the sill.

Down, down the tin soldier fell—three stories onto the street below. It was a terrible fall. He landed headfirst with his gun stuck

between two cobblestones and his leg in the air. The children and the maid ran outside to look for him but they couldn't find him anywhere.

That afternoon, it began to rain. It was a quick, hard rain that filled the gutters. When it was over, two boys came out to play. "Look!" one of them cried. "There's a tin soldier. Let's make him a boat!" So they made a boat out of an old newspaper. Then they set the little tin soldier in the boat and sent him sailing down the gutter.

How fast the little paper boat went! How deep the water seemed! The little tin soldier could not help being frightened. But he bravely stood as straight as he could and held tightly to his gun.

Suddenly the little paper boat was swept into a drain and down a dark tunnel.

"How black it is in here," thought the little tin soldier. "Where am I going, I wonder? It is all the goblin's fault! Oh, if only the little dancer were here with me. Then I would not care even if it were twice as dark!"

Just then a large water rat swam up to the boat. "Where is your passport?" he hissed at the tin solider. "Give it to me at once!" The tin soldier did not reply but grasped his gun more tightly. So the water rat gnashed his teeth and howled, "Stop him! Stop him! He hasn't shown his passport!" But the little paper boat was soon carried away by the current.

Now the tin soldier could see a light ahead. As the boat drew closer to the light, he heard a terrible roaring sound. It was loud enough to strike fear into the bravest heart. You see, the tunnel emptied into a canal. The plunge would be as dangerous for the tin soldier as an enormous waterfall would be for you or me. The little tin soldier was terribly afraid, but he stood as straight as ever and shouldered his gun.

The paper boat tumbled down into the canal. It whirled round and round and filled with water. The tin soldier did not move a muscle. Instead he thought of the pretty little dancer whom he was sure he would never see again. Then he remembered the words of an old military song:

Farewell, soldier, true and brave,
Going toward your cold, dark grave!

Finally the paper boat dissolved in the water, and the little tin soldier sank.

Just then a large fish swam by and swallowed the tin soldier. How dark it was inside the fish's belly—even darker than in the tunnel. But the little tin soldier still stood straight and bravely shouldered his gun.

The fish darted this way and that until the tin soldier felt terribly shaken up. Then, after a time, the fish was still. Next a flash of lightning seemed to pass through the fish, and the little tin soldier found himself in daylight again.

"Why, look!" cried a voice. "Here is the tin soldier!"

You see the fish
had been caught and
taken to market where the cook had bought
him. She brought him back to the kitchen
and had cut him open with a big knife.

The cook picked up the tin soldier between her fingers. Then she carefully carried
him upstairs so everyone could see the amaz-
ing little soldier who had traveled so far in
the belly of a fish.

24

When the cook set the tin soldier on the table, everyone cried in glee and admiration. The tin soldier looked around. To his amazement, he was back in the very room he had started from.

The little boy was there, and so were the other twenty-four tin soldiers, as well as all the rest of the toys. In the corner of the table stood the paper castle. The tin soldier saw that the pretty little dancer was still standing on one leg in the castle door, for she was as steadfast and true as he himself was.

When the little tin soldier saw the dancer, he was so touched that if he could he would have wept tears of tin. But of course, he could not. So he only stared at the little dancer and she stared at him and neither of them spoke.

Just then the little boy picked up the tin
soldier and threw him into the fire. I think
this *really* must have been the red goblin's
doing, for why else would the little boy have
done such a thing?

Flames flared around the little tin soldier.

The heat felt terrible to him, but whether it was the heat of the fire or the warmth of his feelings for the little dancer, he could not say. The bright colors faded from his uniform, but even that might have been from sorrow. He stared at the little dancer and she stared at him. He could feel himself melting away, but he still stood as straight as ever, for he was a brave, true soldier.

Just then the door of the room flew open and a draft of wind picked up the little dancer. She fluttered across the room right into the fire beside the little tin soldier.

Flames blazed around the little dancer and in a flash she was gone. Beside her the tin soldier slowly melted away into a lump of gray metal.

The next morning when the maid cleared away the ashes, all she found of the little tin soldier was a small tin heart. Of the pretty little dancer, nothing was left except her sequin, and that was burned as black as coal.